Artful Reading

Bob Raczka

M̲ MILLBROOK PRESS/MINNEAPOLIS

To Larry & Nancy, two of my favorite book lovers,
with thanks for your enthusiastic support

Millbrook Press, Inc.
A division of Lerner Publishing Group, Inc.
241 First Avenue North
Minneapolis, MN 55401 U.S.A.

Website address: www.lernerbooks.com

Library of Congress Cataloging-in-Publication Data

Raczka, Bob.
    Artful reading / by Bob Raczka.
      p.   cm.
    ISBN: 978-0-8225-6754-7 (lib. bdg. : alk. paper)
    1. Reading in art—Juvenile literature. 2. Painting, Modern—Juvenile literature. I. Title.
    ND1460.R42R33 2008
    700'.557—dc22   2006035083

Manufactured in the United States of America
1 2 3 4 5 6 – JR – 13 12 11 10 09 08

3

Read by
yourself.

August Macke • *Man Reading in the Park* (1914) • Museum Ludwig, Cologne, Germany

Read with each other.

Charles Willson Peale • *Mrs. James Smith and Grandson* (1776)
Smithsonian American Art Museum, Washington, D.C.

Read one good book.
Then read another.

Vincent Van Gogh • *L'Arlésienne: Madame Joseph-Michel Ginoux* (1888 or 1889)
Metropolitan Museum of Art, New York

Read to discover
what something means.

Edgar Degas • *Portrait of Edmond Duranty* (1879) • Glasgow Museums and Art Galleries

Read to escape to a place you can dream.

Dante Gabriel Rossetti • *The Day Dream* (1880) • Victoria and Albert Museum, London

Read the news.

Paul Cézanne • *The Artist's Father* (1866) • National Gallery of Art, Washington, D.C.

Or read
a globe.

Johannes Vermeer • *The Astronomer* (1668) • Musée du Louvre, Paris

Read in a dress.

Jean-Honoré Fragonard • *A Young Girl Reading* (ca. 1776) • National Gallery of Art, Washington, D.C.

Or read in
your robe.

Albrecht Dürer • *The Four Apostles (John & Peter)* (1523–26) • Alte Pinakothek, Munich

Édouard Manet • *The Railway* (1873) • National Gallery of Art, Washington, D.C.

Read while
you wait
for your
train to
come in.

Read to find out
how somebody's been.

Johannes Vermeer • *Woman in Blue Reading a Letter* (1662–63) • Rijksmuseum, Amsterdam

Read in a garden.

Mary Cassatt • *On a Balcony* (1878–79) • Art Institute of Chicago

Read in a house.

Antonello da Messina • *St. Jerome in His Study* (ca. 1475) • The National Gallery, London

Read by the window.

Henri Matisse • *The French Window at Nice* (1919) • Barnes Foundation, Merion, Pennsylvania

Pierre-Auguste Renoir • *Children's Afternoon at Wargemont* (1884)
Staatliche Museen zu Berlin

Read
on the
couch.

Read while you work.

Quentin Massys • *The Moneylender and His Wife* (1514) • Musée du Louvre, Paris

Read while you ride.

Edward Hopper • *Compartment C, Car 293* (1938) • IBM Corporation, Armonk, New York

Milton Avery • *Adolescence* (1947) • Terra Foundation for American Art, Chicago

Read what you *want*. It's for you to decide.

Read when
you're young.

Jean-Baptiste-Siméon Chardin • *Young Schoolmistress* (ca. 1735–36) • The National Gallery, London

Read when you're old.

Attributed to Rembrandt van Rijn • *Rembrandt's Mother* (1629) • Wilton House, Salisbury, UK

Read all the words
you can possibly hold.

Carl Spitzweg • *The Bookworm* (1850) • Milwaukee Public Library

Read to a friend.
That's what friends are for.

Pablo Picasso • *Two Girls Reading* (1934) • University of Michigan Museum of Art, Ann Arbor

Jacob Lawrence • *The Library* (1960) • Smithsonian American Art Museum, Washington, D.C.

Read all
your life
and
you'll
never
be
bored.

ARTISTS AS READERS AND WRITERS

August Macke
(1887–1914) German
To spread new ideas about art, August Macke and a group of his friends published a special book called *Der Blaue Reiter* (The Blue Rider) almanac. It was a collection of artwork and essays on art from all over Europe.

Dante Gabriel Rossetti
(1828–1882) English
Dante Rossetti was a poet as well as a painter. He grew up in London, and as a boy, he spent many hours in the British Museum Reading Room, absorbing as much great literature as he could.

Charles Willson Peale
(1741–1827) American
The boy in this painting, whose name is Campbell Smith, is reading a book called *The Art of Speaking*. His finger is pointing to the words "To be, or not to be" from William Shakespeare's famous play, *Hamlet*.

Paul Cézanne
(1839–1906) French
Because Paul Cézanne's father was a banker, he read a newspaper that was popular with businessmen. But as a little joke, Cézanne painted him reading *L'Evenement*, the newspaper preferred by French artists and writers.

Vincent Van Gogh
(1853–1890) Dutch
Vincent Van Gogh was a great lover of books. He read everything from the plays of William Shakespeare to the fairy tales of Hans Christian Andersen. One of his favorite books was *A Christmas Carol* by Charles Dickens.

Johannes Vermeer
(1632–1675) Dutch
The globe that Johannes Vermeer's astronomer is reading is a globe of the stars, called a celestial globe. This one was made by the famous Dutch globemaker and mapmaker Jodocus Hondius in the year 1600.

Edgar Degas
(1834–1917) French
Edmond Duranty was a good friend of Edgar Degas. Duranty was a novelist, but none of his books ever became very popular. He was also an art critic who wrote favorably about Degas and the other Impressionists.

Jean-Honoré Fragonard
(1732–1806) French
Today we consider Jean Fragonard to be one of the greatest painters of his time. But for many years after he died in 1806, he was forgotten. In fact, he wasn't even mentioned in a history of art that was published in 1873.

*Albrecht Dürer
(1471–1528) German*
In addition to making art, Albrecht Dürer also wrote several books about it. The final three volumes of his "Four Books on Human Proportion," which he worked on all his life, were finally published six months after he died.

*Antonello da Messina
(ca.1430–1479) Sicilian*
Saint Jerome is considered one of the four fathers of the Catholic Church. As da Messina shows us, Saint Jerome is famous for translating the Bible from Hebrew and Aramaic into Latin. This version of the Bible is called the Vulgate.

*Édouard Manet
(1832–1883) French*
One of Édouard Manet's friends, Stéphane Mallarmé, was a poet. Mallarmé did not become well known until he published a translation of Edgar Allan Poe's famous poem, "The Raven." The poem was illustrated by Manet.

*Henri Matisse
(1869–1954) French*
Henri Matisse wrote and illustrated a book called *Jazz*, which was published in 1947, when he was seventy-seven years old. He illustrated it with colorful cut-paper collages, and the text is in his own handwriting.

*Johannes Vermeer
(1632–1675) Dutch*
During his lifetime, Johannes Vermeer (also known as Jan) completed very few paintings. In fact, only thirty-five of his confirmed works have survived to this day. But of those paintings, seven show women reading or writing letters.

*Pierre-Auguste Renoir
(1841–1919) French*
Renoir and his wife Aline had three children, all of them boys. Jean, their second son, became a successful filmmaker. In 1962 he wrote a touching biography of his father called *Renoir, My Father*.

*Mary Cassatt
(1844–1926) American*
Mary Cassatt often used her sister, Lydia, as a model for her paintings. In 2001 the author Harriet Scott Chessman published a novel about Mary's relationship with her sister called *Lydia Cassatt Reading the Morning Paper*.

*Quentin Massys
(also spelled Messys)
(1466–1530) Belgian*
The moneylender's wife, who is turning the pages of a religious book, is not the only person reading in this painting. If you look closely at the mirror on the table, you can see the reflection of a man reading by a window.

*Edward Hopper
(1882–1967) American*
The theme of Edward Hopper's work seems to be loneliness. He often painted people reading, lost in their own little worlds—just as we get lost in our own little worlds when we look at his paintings.

*Carl Spitzweg
(1808–1885) German*
Ever since Carl Spitzweg painted *The Bookworm*, engravings and posters of it have been popular among people who love to read. Appropriately enough, the original painting now hangs in the Milwaukee Public Library.

*Milton Avery
(1885–1965) American*
Milton Avery was a great family man, and he often entertained his wife, Sally, and their daughter, March, by reading out loud to them. His favorite authors included Herman Melville and Henry David Thoreau.

*Pablo Picasso
(1881–1973) Spanish*
According to the *Guinness Book of World Records*, Pablo Picasso produced more paintings than any other artist ever known–about 13,500 in all. He also created nearly 34,000 book illustrations.

*Jean-Baptiste-Siméon Chardin
(1699–1779) French*
Because Jean Chardin painted scenes from everyday life, many of them were made into engravings and sold to the public. The engravings often came with poems, which were written by the engravers to "explain" the pictures.

*Jacob Lawrence
(1917–2000) American*
The library was an important place to Jacob Lawrence. As a boy, he learned to paint at the Harlem Art Workshop, which was located inside the New York Public Library. Later, he used the library to do research for his paintings.

Rembrandt Harmenszoon van Rijn (ca. 1606–1669) Dutch
There is controversy as to whether Rembrandt actually painted this portrait. Current scholars think the master may have rendered the Bible but that it was mainly painted by Rembrandt's friend Jan Lievens.